Blue Sky
studios.

epic

The Junior Novel

HarperFestival is an imprint of HarperCollins Publishers.

Epic © 2013 Twentieth Century Fox Film Corporation.
HarperCollins Children's Books, a division of HarperCollins Publishers, 10 East 53rd Street, New York, NY 10022.
www.harpercollinschildrens.com
Library of Congress catalog card number: 2012955881
ISBN 978-0-06-220995-5
Designed by David Neuhaus

13 14 15 16 17   LP/BR   10 9 8 7 6 5 4 3 2 1
❖
First Edition

Blue Sky studios

epic

The Junior Novel

Adapted by Annie Auerbach

HARPER FESTIVAL

An Imprint of HarperCollinsPublishers

Blue Sky
studios.

epic

The Junior Novel

1

A hummingbird flew quickly through the trees, its hurried sound breaking the calmness of the forest. The bird twisted and turned through the leaves and around the branches as it tried to escape the nasty grackle chasing it down.

Suddenly a louder sound could be heard.

Something was breaking through the thick under-brush. Was it a bear? A wolf?

No—scarier! It was a scientist! Armed with goggles, binoculars, and a backpack, Professor Bomba looked toward the bird fight above him. He could hear it, but he couldn't see it through the leafy branches. He pulled out a remote control and pushed a button.

At that moment, several tree-mounted, wireless cameras came to life, swinging in all directions. Bomba held his breath as he looked at the screen on his remote control. One of the cameras caught the fighting birds rushing past. Using the device, Bomba stumbled along the forest floor, following as best he could. He heard a single *chirp*, and then something fell through the branches.

Bomba rushed over and bent down, disheartened to see an injured hummingbird lying on the forest

floor. He flipped down his goggles and adjusted them so he could see more clearly. To his fascination, Bomba spotted a tiny saddle on its back. Bomba felt sorry for the bird, but was also elated that he may have found proof of a civilization of tiny people. He had yet to see them, but he was convinced they were real.

In fact, they were close by . . .

The grackle whirled around the high branches, hunting for prey. The rider aboard the shiny, black bird was only two inches high, but he was still a nasty piece of work called a Boggan. Boggans were brutish, bug-like creatures who wanted to take over the forest and ruin it.

An arrow shot from the Boggan's bow, speeding

toward its target: one of the Jinn. The Jinn were human-looking creatures, also only two inches tall. Jinn had varied appearances and were able to camouflage themselves in the forest. Unlike the evil Boggans, the Jinn believed in the protection of the forest, not the destruction.

A group of special and brave Jinn soldiers called the Leafmen believed it was their duty to defend the forest against evil forces. They moved like samurai warriors and rode hummingbirds as if they were fighter jets. It was one of these Leafmen that was currently under attack from a Boggan. His name was Nod.

Wearing a helmet, armor, and carrying a sword, Nod ran along a thin branch when suddenly *thwack!* The Boggan arrow pierced the branch near Nod's heel. The arrow was poisonous. Instantly, a seeping

wound formed at the impact point of the tree, and decay began to spread.

Nod looked up to see two more Boggans fly in—and another arrow, heading straight for him. Just before it made its mark, three hummingbirds swooped in. Leafmen were aboard them, primed for battle.

Ronin, the leader of the Leafmen, skillfully turned his bird upside down as he flew past. He cut the airborne Boggan arrow in two with his blade. Nod was safe once again!

Of course, this just made the Boggans angrier. But although they were dangerous, the Boggans lacked military precision and training. They dove and swarmed from random directions, firing arrows at Nod, all of them missing their mark.

Ronin flew alongside Nod. "Need a lift?"

"I don't need your help," Nod said confidently.

"You're running out of branch there, buddy," Ronin pointed out.

Nod shook his head. "I told you, I got this all worked out—"

The Boggan's grackle suddenly veered over and snatched Nod in one of his talons!

2

"**H**elllllppppp!" shouted Nod.

In an instant, Ronin leaped onto the grackle. Dedicated and well respected, Ronin wouldn't think twice about putting his own life on the line for someone he cared about. He fought the Boggan rider, while Nod dangled below by one leg.

"Why aren't you with your group?" Ronin asked Nod, while still fighting the Boggan.

"I fly faster alone," Nod replied. Carefree and sometimes reckless, Nod was all about having a good time.

"How do you not get this? You're not the only one on this team, you know," said Ronin.

"So? Yell at one of them for a change!" suggested Nod.

Ronin lifted up his sword and blocked as the Boggan took a swipe at him. Then Ronin kicked the Boggan off the grackle, saving Nod . . . again.

"You know how important today is?" Ronin asked Nod. "Now get a bird and get back to Moonhaven or you're done. I'm not coming after you again."

Nod folded his arms, still dangling from the grackle's talons. "You know what? I'll save you the trouble. I quit."

Ronin took off, leaving Nod to find his own way down.

Meanwhile, seventeen-year-old Mary Katherine sat in the back of a cab. After years away, M.K. was *not* looking forward to her visit home to see her father. Eventually, the cab came to a stop in front of an old, dilapidated house.

"That's not a house, that's termites holding hands," said the cab driver. After a moment, he quickly added, "No offense."

"Don't worry, I'll be fine," said M.K., getting out of the cab.

"Call if you need a quick getaway, kid," said the driver and sped off.

M.K. stared at the house in front of her. *It was probably beautiful once*, she thought. But now paint peeled like sunburned skin, the house numbers had fallen off, and the rain gutters were so full of dirt that weeds sprouted out of them. M.K. sighed deeply, walked to the front door, and knocked. When there was no response, she gently pushed the door open.

If the outside of the house had been taken over by nature, the inside seemed to be taken over by a mad scientist with an affection for clutter. Every inch was crammed with scribbled notes, bell jars, scientific drawings, insect collections, and all kinds of home-made scientific gear.

M.K. glimpsed a small display case filled with sharpened twigs and nutshell fragments. They sort of looked like arrows and armor.

What on earth . . . ? she thought.

Just then, Professor Bomba scurried past her, down the hall.

"Let me see," he muttered to himself, not seeing M.K. at all. "Made of polished acorn shell and thin leather."

M.K. followed him and found him at a microscope, placing something under it to view.

"Hi, Dad."

Bomba was startled. "Mary Katherine! You're here."

"Yeah," she replied as he enveloped her in a big hug.

"I didn't realize today was today," he said.

M.K. grimaced. "It always is."

"But here you are, so it must be," continued Bomba. "Today, I mean. Makes sense." He quickly

changed the subject. "Let me look at you. You look just like your mother!"

An uncomfortable silence hung in the air as each of them thought of M.K.'s mother, who had passed away.

"There actually are a few things I want to talk to you about," M.K. started to say, but she was interrupted by a sudden *bark*.

"Ozzy! Look who's back!" Bomba said to the pug that scampered in. With three legs and one eye, the dog had seen better days.

M.K. was amazed. "Ozzy? He's still alive?"

Ozzy barked. Then sneezed. Then drooled.

"Well, most of him," replied Bomba. "He may be down to three legs, but he'll make a break for it the first chance he gets." He yelled into the dog's ear. "Ozzy, go say hi!"

"Here, boy," M.K. called encouragingly.

Ozzy ran straight . . . past her.

Bomba shrugged. "His depth perception's a little off, and he has a tendency to run in circles. But that was closer than usual. He remembers you!" He gestured for her to follow him up the stairs. "I have a little surprise for you."

Bomba opened a bedroom door. "Here we are. Your old room!"

M.K. was almost speechless. The room was princess pink and perfect for a little girl, which she wasn't anymore.

"It's like I never left," M.K. said, a bit horrified.

"All your things are here," her father continued. "You've got your dolls, your pictures. . . ." He looked at her and finally realized that she wasn't a little girl anymore. "Well, it's good to

have you home, Mary Katherine."

"Actually, I go by 'M.K.' now," she said.

"Oh. M.K.? I like that," said Bomba. "It's more . . . grown-up."

At that moment, a beeping sound pierced the air.

"What's that?" asked M.K.

Bomba flipped a switch on his belt sensor to stop the beeping. "That was just one of my sensors," he explained excitedly. "Today is actually a highly unusual day because there's both a full moon tonight and the summer solstice, which only coincide every hundred years or so." Finally, he took a breath. "Well, you probably want some time to settle in. Make yourself at home, Mary, uh, M.K."

Bomba walked out of the room, gently closing the door behind him. Then he tripped and tumbled down the stairs. "I'm okay!" he shouted.

M.K. sighed. She sat on the tiny bed, her knees almost hitting her chin. In every way, she didn't fit.

Coming home was the worst idea ever, she thought to herself.

Ronin and two other Leafmen skillfully rode their hummingbirds back toward Moonhaven— the city of the Jinn. It was a beautiful place at the water's source, formed out of living plants and stone. As Ronin flew closer, other Jinn came out and welcomed them back.

After dismounting, Ronin immediately sought a meeting with Queen Tara.

Beautiful and strong, Tara was not only the queen, she was the life force of the forest, and the only one with the power to give and restore life. It was her job to preside over the forest with respect and compassion. She also had a soft spot for Ronin.

Ronin found her in a lovely, shaded grove and kneeled down. "Your Majesty, we need to discuss today's ceremony. Boggans have crossed our borders again, and—"

"You're not getting enough sunshine," the queen interrupted.

Ronin looked up at her, confused. Then he realized Tara was talking to a sprout, whose leaves were drooping.

The queen laughed gently and continued talking to the sprout. "Well, I think he looks silly kneeling there, too, but I can't get him to stop doing it."

Ronin stood up and began again. "I think the Boggans are scouting our defenses. You know they'd do anything to stop you from choosing an heir. But don't worry. I've got a plan."

"When we were kids, he wasn't so serious," Queen Tara told the flower. "And he had the sweetest smile." With a swirl of her hand, the tree canopy swayed, letting a beam of sunlight fall on the sprout.

Ronin sighed. "Would you like to hear my plan?" When she didn't answer, he continued. "Instead of a public ceremony, I go in with a small platoon. Pretend we're stopping for a drink. We grab a pod,

and bring it back to you. It blooms. We're in, we're out."

Queen Tara shook her head. "It doesn't work that way. I can't choose unless I'm there. It's about the feeling. I get it from the pods. I get it from the forest. I get it from all of us. Don't you have feelings, Ronin?"

"Yes," replied Ronin. "I *feel* this is a bad idea. The Boggans are determined and deadly."

"I'm not completely helpless," said the queen.

"I am aware," said Ronin. "But you're the life of the forest. Looking after you is my duty."

"Is that the only reason you do it?" she teased.

Ronin resisted the urge to smile. "Isn't that reason enough?"

The queen relented. "I know you're concerned. But this is the one day in a hundred years I can

choose an heir. You look out for me, and I'll look out for the rest of us." She gave Ronin one last smile, and he finally smiled back.

But as she left, Ronin's face darkened with worry. He was distressed about the potential danger ahead.

Beyond the forest border, an area of wilted weeds and decaying trees comprised the place known as Wrathwood. There, inside a large, rotting stump was the underground home of the Boggans.

A Boggan general named Dagda made his way through Wrathwood to meet with his boss. Dagda

was known for being big and scary. His boss, Mandrake, the leader of the Boggans, was even bigger and scarier! Mandrake was the kind of guy who would pull the wings off a fly just for fun. He had the ability to bring destruction to anything he touched.

Dagda found Mandrake stirring a pool of simmering ooze with a club.

"Did you find the location of the ceremony?" Mandrake asked.

"Yes, sir," answered Dagda. "But it's way outside our borders."

"Good. Then they'll be totally surprised," said Mandrake with a lethal smile. "The Leafmen think they can keep us contained. They try and try and try, but they just can't stop the rot."

He lifted the club and watched it drip with sizzling poison. He held up a large, green leaf and

touched the club to it. The leaf instantly disintegrated into ash. This pleased him. "Isn't decay just as natural as growth? Isn't gray just as lovely as green?"

"Doesn't 'fungus' start with 'fun'?" added Dagda. Mandrake didn't laugh. At all.

"Today we fight back," Mandrake declared, ignoring Dagda's last comment. The Boggan leader was tired of hiding in the shadows. "If their queen dies before choosing an heir, the forest dies with her. And who doesn't want *that*?" He looked at Dagda, expecting an answer.

Dagda fidgeted nervously. "The . . . Leafmen?"

Mandrake took an arrow and placed a drop of the poisonous liquid on it. He handed it carefully to Dagda.

Dagda took the arrow, understanding the importance of what was to come. "I will not disappoint you . . . Dad."

Not too far away, another dad was busy making plans, too. But he was up in a tree, adjusting a mini-camera.

M.K. wandered outside the house looking for her father. "Dad? Is this a good time to talk?" she asked, when she found him.

"Hold on," said Bomba. "I'll be right down—"

WHUMP! He fell out of the tree, and the camera was hurled across the yard.

Bomba got up from the ground and called to his dog. "Ozzy, Ozzy! Fetch the camera!"

Ozzy didn't do "fetch." Instead, he tried to scratch an itch, then tipped over.

"Why do you have security cameras anyway?" asked M.K. "Do people around here steal old newspapers?"

"Oh, no, they're not security cameras," Bomba explained. "I have an extensive network all through the forest. I don't know how much your mother told you about my work."

"Um, nothing, just that you have a delusional belief in an advanced society of tiny people living in the woods, and it ruined your career, not to mention your marriage," said M.K. "Or something."

Bomba tried to cover up feeling hurt. With a forced smile, he said, "Your mother had a wonderful sense of humor." Then he added, "But I'm not delusional. They're out there—a civilization that's thrived in these woods for who knows how long. And I will prove it!"

He ran inside the house and retrieved his mp3 player and a small portable speaker. He scrolled through a playlist, then clicked on a selection. Whining sounds came through the speaker.

"You have bat sounds? Why?" asked M.K.

"To study them," replied her father. "I was trying to identify the frequencies that draw bats to gather with their own kind. So I slowed the sounds down, put them through some proprietary filters, and guess what I heard?"

"Voices?" M.K. asked hesitantly, worried she would be right.

"Yes!" Bomba exclaimed. He played the slowed-down sounds. It sounded like faint whispers. "Isn't that cool?" he said.

M.K. took a deep breath. "Okay. If tiny men are flying around in the forest, how come I've never seen them?"

"That's easy!" Bomba declared. "It's the same reason we can't hear them—they move too fast, like insects!"

"Have *you* ever seen one?" asked M.K.

"I, ah . . . ," began Bomba. "You know what? Just because you haven't seen something doesn't mean it's not there."

M.K. was losing patience with her father's stories of the tiny men living in the woods. It was time to get serious. "Okay, we need to talk, for real. Dad, look, I'm almost old enough to be on my own anyway, so I think it would be better if I just . . ."

Suddenly Bomba understood. "You don't want to live here? That's what you want?"

"No," said M.K., trying to fight back tears. "It's not what I want. I want you to stop all this . . . and be normal. I want a dad who's not—"

Beep! Beep! Beep! One of Bomba's alarms flashed.

Bomba was giddy with excitement. "Oh, this is big. This is a big thing going on. Let me just find, uh . . ."

M.K. watched him rush around, collecting things. "Where are you going?"

"I'm just going to investigate. Something must be happening," said Bomba, unable to contain his anticipation. "You have to catch these things in the moment. Otherwise, you miss a chance that could be gone forever."

"You're missing a chance right now!" said M.K., exasperated. "Are you even listening?"

"Look, you've got to believe me," Bomba said. "I'm so close. All I need is one little breakthrough. This could be it!" At the doorway, he turned and faced his daughter. "I'll clear this all up when I get back. I promise you."

"Sure, Dad, I'll be here," she said sadly, "in reality."

A few minutes later, M.K. taped a note to one of

her father's computer monitors. Ozzy appeared and nudged her leg.

"Bye, Ozzy. It's not you," she said to the dog, petting him. Then she dragged her suitcase outside the front door and tried to call for a cab. But she couldn't get a signal on her cell phone.

Just then, the dog bolted outside, heading straight for the woods.

"Ozzy! Heel! Stop! Play dead!" shouted M.K. "How are you so fast on three legs? Ozzy!"

She raced after him, almost tripping over her suitcase. It fell from the stoop and tumbled into the bushes. M.K. began to turn back to get it, but then noticed Ozzy dashing into the forest, with no intention of stopping.

"Ozzy!" she called again. When he didn't come back, M.K. knew she only had one choice: follow him.

5

Ronin flew aboard his bird to the part of Moonhaven where the royal barge was departing from. When it was time, the dragonflies fluttered their wings and took flight, pulling the barge with Queen Tara onboard. Ronin and the Leafmen flew close by to escort the barge, and ensure the queen's safety.

As the barge moved, flowers bloomed and bent toward Queen Tara. Leaves bowed, vines stretched out, and the connection between the queen and the forest was obvious.

Before long, the dragonflies landed on marsh grass at the edge of a small pond. High above, Ronin and the Leafmen set up a perimeter, staying on high alert. Here and there, Jinn peeked out of the undergrowth. They couldn't help their curiosity during this momentous occasion.

A mother and daughter Jinn, both flower-like in appearance, looked on.

"Isn't she pretty?" said the mother.

"She's awesome! She moved those trees with her mind!" exclaimed the daughter. "Mom, can I be queen when I grow up?"

Her mother smiled. "Oh, honey, it doesn't work

that way. Queen Tara chooses a special pod and nurtures it until it blooms. Then we get our new queen."

Nearby, at the pond's edge, a slug and a snail nervously watched the queen approach.

"She's coming!" cried Grub, the snail. He looked at the slug, adding, "I implore you, don't do anything to embarrass me, or it could ruin my chances of being a Leafman!"

"Why do you want to be a Leafman?" wondered Mub, the slug. "They've got to wear uniforms. Me? I like to let it all hang free." He jiggled his belly, rippling it up and down.

Grub grimaced. "Don't do that! EVER!"

The queen stepped up to them. "Gentlemen."

Grub snapped to attention. "Your Majesty," he said, filled with embarrassment.

"It's all right. You can relax," began Queen Tara,

then she looked at the many lotus-like pods floating on the water. "It's a very nice-looking group of pods. I might have a hard time picking one. Do you have a favorite?"

Mub and Grub looked at each other.

"Well, Your Majesty," began Grub. "We've had quite the debate—"

"Really gone back and forth," added Mub.

"With so many factors to consider: color, density, roundness. Can't be too hasty!" said Grub.

Mub dropped an extra-large pod on a lily pad. "Boom! Right here. Biggest in the bunch!"

"Well," said the queen, "that's *one* way to go." She moved on, eyes closed, passing a hand over a row of pods until finally her hand trembled slightly. She opened her eyes and saw an ordinary-looking pod. "How about that one?"

Mub whispered to Grub, "That one? For real? But it's—"

"It's perfect!" said Grub. "Excellent choice, Your Majesty. Sometimes the biggest one isn't the best one." Then to Mub, he added, "I told you. She doesn't like gaudy. Unlike you, she's got class!"

Queen Tara felt confident with her decision. "This is it. This is the one."

From his view above, Ronin scanned the forest. *The sooner this is over, the better,* he thought to himself.

Suddenly, a leaf near him started to decay. He immediately knew something wasn't right. He fired an arrow at a branch, and a Boggan that was hiding behind the bark fell.

The tree shuddered, as if coming to life, and then Ronin's worst fear came true: an all-out Boggan attack!

6

Ronin and the Leafmen reacted instantly and spurred their hummingbirds on. The birds were great in battle because they could fly backward or forward. This gave the Leafmen the opportunity to face every direction to fend off the surprise Boggan attack. Another group of Leafmen split off and made

a protective, dome-like shield over the queen.

"Your Majesty, get to the barge!" Ronin told Queen Tara.

The queen took off toward the barge, as the Leafmen advanced on the Boggans erupting from the tree. Queen Tara was almost at the barge when she spotted the daughter Jinn and her mother running away from a Boggan. The queen summoned a branch that swatted the Boggan away.

"I told you she was awesome!" the daughter said to her mother.

A horde of Boggans ran toward Mub and Grub.

"This it it, Mub!" said Grub, preparing for a fight. "My chance to be a Leaf—"

The Boggans ran right over them, ignoring the slug and the snail.

Queen Tara looked at the water and gasped. She

saw pods disappearing, being yanked underwater from below. She began to run, and as she did, leaves bent over her to shield her.

But the Boggan arrows pierced the leaves, burning holes through them. The decaying power of the Boggans was doing its best to wreck the forest.

So as Queen Tara passed Boggan-wounded leaves or stems, her touch restored them. She also used the forest itself: commanding vines to grab Boggans off their mounts, or asking branches to bend to block the Boggans' paths.

In an upper tree branch, Mandrake paused to assess the attack. Dagda flew up to him.

"We had numbers, and we had surprise," said Dagda. "How are we losing?"

But Mandrake was focused on the task at hand. "You get the pod, and I'm going to get the queen." He

spurred his bird and swooped down, heading toward Queen Tara. Dagda struggled to follow behind.

On the ground, Tara clutched the pod close but stopped short when a giant, snarling Boggan blocked her path. The daughter Jinn was close by and looked at her trapped hero. Then the young girl pulled back a branch, which snapped forward, effectively taking out the Boggan blocking Tara.

"Nice one!" the queen said to the girl. "You're stealing my moves, kid!" Then the queen turned to a Leafman. "Take her to safety. I have to lead them away from the crowd."

"You're totally my hero!" the girl called to Queen Tara.

As Queen Tara ran toward Ronin, leaves and branches formed a makeshift staircase in front of her. She leaped onto his bird and held on.

"Okay, so maybe you were right," she said to Ronin over the sound of the wind.

"Remind me to gloat later!" replied Ronin.

At that moment, a wretched screech pierced the air.

Ronin looked up to see Mandrake and Dagda bearing down. Dagda fired, and Ronin deflected. Dagda fired again and again, but Ronin blocked each arrow.

Mandrake drew his bow.

Ronin drew his bow and shot at Dagda.

Mandrake fired an arrow a split second before Ronin's arrow found its mark—taking down Dagda. Ronin thought he'd foiled the attack, but for Mandrake the battle was far from over. . . .

At the same time, M.K. stumbled along in another part of the forest, feeling lost and frustrated. Somewhere up ahead, she heard Ozzy barking. As she turned toward the sound she spotted a tiny glow. It was the queen floating toward the ground. M.K. kneeled down for a closer look. The queen had been wounded. Since the queen could no longer protect the pod, she breathed her energy into it and tossed it up to M.K.

As soon as M.K. caught it, a connection was made and there was a sudden flash of light. M.K. hurtled through the air as if hit by a hurricane-force gust of wind. Sound and motion slowed down and the human world and the world of the

Jinn began to smash together.

"Aaaaaahhhh!" cried M.K., as she flew among swirling leaves.

Finally she landed, bouncing on soft moss. She was Jinn-sized now, though not yet aware of it. She felt something and looked at her arm. The pod's tendrils clung to her.

Then she saw Queen Tara.

"Take the pod to Nim Galuu," the queen said quietly. "It's the life of the forest." After saying it, she magically faded away.

"**W**hat did the queen say to you?" Ronin asked M.K.

M.K. furrowed her eyebrows. "Something about glue. Or a canoe."

"Nim Galuu," Ronin said.

"The scrollkeeper?" asked Ronin's lieutenant,

thinking of the wise man of that name.

Ronin thought for a minute and then gave instructions to his lieutenant. "I'll take the pod to Nim's. Mandrake will be looking for a cluster, not a Leafman traveling alone. You and the others go back to Moonhaven. Keep everyone safe."

As the other Leafmen took off, M.K. turned to Ronin. "Who are you people? Is this some kind of reenactment or something?" She spotted a jumbo-sized honeybee pass by. "That's a big bug."

"It's about average, actually," Ronin said.

M.K. laughed. "Then *I'm* tiny?" She looked around and then the truth dawned on her. "Oh no. Oh no. No, no, no!"

"Look, I'm not sure why the queen brought you here either," said Ronin. "But she gave you that pod, so you're going to have to come with me." He

reached for her, but she pulled away.

"Make me big," said M.K.

"Excuse me?" said Ronin.

"I'm not going anywhere until you make me big again!" insisted M.K.

"I don't do magic. Talk to Nim Galuu about that. He might know something," said Ronin. He tried to grab the pod from her, but Mub stepped in his way.

"Whoa, whoa, not so fast, soldier boy," said Mub. "You do not yank on a pod!"

M.K. couldn't believe her ears. "Talking snails!"

"Actually, he's a snail, I'm a slug," Mub clarified. "No shell over here, baby. It just slows me down."

Grub piped up. "We are the official pod caretakers, sir."

"It can't survive without us," said Mub.

"We keep it moist," said Grub.

"Moist is what we do!" Mub added proudly.

"You're kidding," said Ronin.

Mub and Grub didn't say a word.

"You're not kidding?" Ronin sighed. "Fine."

Ronin turned to M.K. and said, "Better get on the bird. Good seats are going fast."

"Bird," said M.K., as she caught sight of their mode of transportation. "Of course." She climbed aboard the bird, wondering if the day could possibly get any weirder.

From far away, it looked just like a flock of birds swooping around trees, happily flitting through the forest. But a closer look would reveal that a race was underway!

A sparrow rocketed past with Nod aboard. He piloted the bird skillfully, moving up through a pack

of other birds, each with a jockey aboard. They all jostled, bumped, and snapped with their beaks during the dangerous race. Lining the branches were shady-looking Jinn, who were placing bets.

A couple of rough jockeys pulled up to Nod.

Nod shouted, "I'm telling you this is where I belong!"

"You belong in the back of the pack," yelled one of the jockeys.

"I mean racing—the best man wins, no other rules. Nobody telling you what to do," Nod shouted.

Another jockey cried out, "You talk too much. And you're not winning this race!"

Nod just smiled, then shouted, "Sorry, can't hear you, going too fast!" And he darted ahead.

"Final lap!" called the announcer.

One of the racers caught up to Nod. "You know

what will happen if you win?"

"Yeah," said Nod. "You'll lose."

With that, Nod pulled ahead and won the race. The crowd cheered.

Unfortunately, as soon as the race was over, Nod found himself getting roughed up by a couple of nasty jockeys. A frowning, toad-like Jinn named Bufo watched.

"Nod, you know I like you," began Bufo.

"I like you, too," Nod said.

"And yet, you don't do what we agreed," said Bufo. "We agreed that you would lose, but then you won."

"I can't help it if I'm fast," replied Nod. "If you want me to lose, you've got to give me some better competition."

Bufo smiled. Sort of. "I admire your independent

spirit, Nod. I'll miss that." He turned to one of his men. "Feed him to something. A snake would be good."

Nod's eyes grew wide. He didn't really want to be some animal's lunch.

"Nah, snakes just swallow you whole," said a voice.

It was Ronin!

"Now, if you put him in a hornet's nest, *that's* a show!" Ronin said, his sword drawn.

Bufo rolled his eyes. "Oh, look. It's Ronin, defender of the weak. Pooper of parties. Here to ruin the fun."

"I didn't ruin all of it," corrected Ronin. "I let you hit him."

"Twice," Nod added.

Ronin motioned to Bufo. "Hop along now, little froggy."

Bufo and his men did just that. They all knew they were no match for Ronin.

Once they were gone, Nod immediately tried to get the upper hand. "Are you here to beg me to come back? Because I'm not going to do it. You said some very mean things."

"I didn't come for you," Ronin said. "The Boggans attacked, and the pod is in great danger."

Nod froze. "Ronin, I'm sorry. I should have been there."

"This isn't about you. I'm just here to get birds," said Ronin. "If we don't get the pod to Nim Galuu's, the forest will die."

In that instant, Nod finally wanted to help. It was time for him to grow up and take on some responsibility. "Let me grab my saddle."

"What? No, I didn't ask for help," said Ronin.

"Really? Because it sounds like you could use a rider with my—"

"Ability to absorb punches?" finished Ronin. "The situation's desperate. Let's not make it hopeless."

Just then, M.K. yelled. Ronin and Nod turned to see her upside down in slime and tangled in the bird's reins. Ronin and Nod looked at one another and instantly agreed that Nod would come along on the journey.

A few minutes later, the group was on the move. Ronin steered his hummingbird with Mub and Grub riding with him. Behind them was a sparrow with Nod and M.K., who wore the pod like a backpack.

Nod looked back at M.K., instead of in front of him. "Hey, I'm Nod, by the way."

"Hi," replied M.K. "Could you just face the way the bird's driving?"

"Don't worry, she practically flies herself," said Nod.

Ronin's stern voice interrupted them. "Nod, perch your bird."

In front of them was a vast meadow, laid to waste. Dead trees, brown grass, and ashen earth covered the once-fertile ground.

"What did that?" asked M.K.

"Mandrake," said Ronin. "He's on the march for Moonhaven. This is what the entire forest will look like unless this pod blooms."

M.K. looked at the pod, now fully appreciating the importance of what they were doing.

Above, a lone starling circled the sky, a Boggan mounted on it.

"We have to go around," Ronin said, pulling his bird's reins.

"Just for one scout?" asked Nod. He just wanted to go through the meadow.

"Ever see just one Boggan?" Ronin pointed out.

Nod ignored Ronin's warning and flew out into the meadow.

Drawing the attention of the camouflaged Boggans, the meadow then exploded with starlings, rising from the underbrush, a Boggan mounted on every one. Nod and Ronin pulled back on their birds' reins and then dove toward the ground.

As soon as the group hit the ground, they hopped off their birds and led them on foot under the cover of the brush. Ronin shepherded them toward the safety of a hollow log.

Just then, a starling dive-bombed Nod and M.K., cutting them off from the others. The

Boggan on the bird's back shrieked.

It was M.K.'s first glimpse of a Boggan up close, and she was paralyzed with fear. The Boggan aimed an arrow. Was this the end for M.K.?

Nod grabbed M.K.'s hand, yanking her out of the path of the deadly arrow. They tumbled into a pit. The starling passed, not seeing where they went.

"What *was* that thing?" exclaimed M.K.

"You've never seen a Boggan?" asked Nod. "Someone

had a happy childhood. Come on, let's regroup."

"You mean up there? With those things?" said M.K. "They almost killed us."

Nod spotted something behind her. "Don't turn around. Walk toward me slowly."

Instead, M.K. whirled around quickly and saw a dark shape with beady eyes. At first, she was frightened, and then it came into the light.

There stood an adorable field mouse, grooming its face with its paws.

"Aww!" said M.K. "Hi, mousie. Look at its wittle hands, and its wittle whiskers."

The mouse bared its super-sharp teeth and let out a roar. M.K. suddenly understood that what might be cute when you're human-sized can be deadly when you're two inches tall!

M.K. screamed, and the mouse charged. M.K.

and Nod ran to the side of the pit. Nod leaped up to another level, as if he were a cricket. "Jump!" he instructed.

"I can't jump that high!" said M.K. But when she turned and saw the mouse barreling at her, she screamed again, and leaped. She was amazed at how high she could jump. "Did you see what I just did?!"

As the mouse charged again, M.K. jumped with confidence—only to hit her head on a root sticking out. She fell hard and now was out cold.

"Great," Nod said with a sigh. So he ran up the wall and backflipped, landing on the mouse's tail.

The mouse started running, going after M.K., but Nod held it back by the tail.

That is, until the mouse whipped its tail, body slamming Nod. The mouse snarled, then crouched, ready for the kill.

Just then, Ronin dropped in. Using his sword, he sliced off one tiny millimeter of the mouse's whisker. The creature yipped and scurried off.

"They have very sensitive whiskers," Ronin said with a shrug.

"You know, I had this," Nod said.

"Sorry. From my angle, it looked like it had you," Ronin pointed out. He walked over to M.K. and woke her up. "Are you all right?"

M.K. still felt woozy. "Dad? I had the most messed-up dream. There were talking slugs and tiny soldiers and—" She spotted Ronin, Mub, and Grub. "Aw, mannnn," she said, disappointed.

"Let's move," ordered Ronin. He whistled, and his bird flew to his side. "New seating arrangement," he said to M.K. "You're with me."

M.K. thanked him. She thought Ronin seemed

more in control than Nod, at least when it came to keeping yourself alive.

"You're with the slugs," Ronin told Nod.

"Disgusting," Nod said with a sneer.

As Ronin and M.K. walked off, Mub got right up into Nod's face.

"Do you and I have a problem?" Mub said.

Nod was confused. "Uh, I don't think so."

"What was that over there? A little chitchat? That's real cute," said Mub. "You trying to jump in?"

"What are we talking about??" asked Nod.

Mub rippled his gelatinous bulk. "There's a code. Amongst men. It goes something like this: I saw her first."

Nod's eyebrows furrowed. "You're a slug."

"So?" Mub replied defensively. "You think she'd want you? Look at yourself." He leaned in. "Oh, that's

right, you can't—because your eyeballs are stuck all the way *inside* your head!"

Mub and Grub snickered.

"What's wrong, flat face?" teased Mub. "Are you going to cry? Do you want me to call your flat-faced mommy?"

"You know, you're not insulting me," Nod told him. "You're just grossing me out."

Mub stretched his eyestalks right into Nod's face. "You've been warned." Then he poked Nod in the eye.

"Ow!"

10

Mandrake and the Boggans moved through the forest spreading blight, destroying as much as they could. Mandrake perched himself on a tree stump when Bufo was marched in by two Boggan guards.

"Hey, if this is a bad time, I can come back when you're done gardening," Bufo said.

Mandrake gained his composure and turned toward his visitor. "I bet you're wondering why I invited you here."

"I was frog-marched here at spear point. How is that 'invited'?" said Bufo.

Mandrake shrugged. "We let you keep your legs."

"Comedy. Terrific," said Bufo. "Funny psychopath."

Mandrake cut to the chase. "There are rumors that the Leafman Ronin was at your place of business. And that he may have rescued a royal pod."

"Real smooth," Bufo said to Mandrake. "You attacked the pod selection ceremony, but let the pod get away. Plus, your idiot general gets himself mulched!"

"That idiot general was my son!" thundered Mandrake.

Bufo gulped. "Of course he was. He had your . . . good looks. And your . . . healthy . . . gray complexion and forgiving nature—"

"Shut up," Mandrake commanded. "What's it going to be, Bufo? Are you going to talk or are you going to croak? Where are they taking the pod?"

Bufo was terrified and felt he had no choice. He told Mandrake what he wanted to know.

11

M.K. held the pod in her lap as she and Ronin sat atop their bird as it hopped from branch to branch. They would briefly fly through the forest, and then land on a branch to survey the path ahead. Nod landed awkwardly next to them.

M.K. gestured to Nod. "Why is he even with us?"

she asked Ronin. "He's not helping."

Ronin turned to her. "Well, when he's not being an idiot, he's a pretty decent flier. Could be one of the best. Plus, his father was my friend. So I do what I can. Many leaves, one tree."

"What does that mean?" asked M.K.

"We're all individuals, but part of a community," Ronin explained.

"Maybe you're part of it. But I'm kind of on my own," M.K. said sadly.

"No one's on their own," Ronin said. He pointed to Nod. "Not even him."

Moments later, the small group flew down and perched near a massive, old oak tree. It was hollow, thick, grand, and welcoming, as if its branches seemed to be trying to embrace the whole forest. Huge numbers of Jinn filed into the entrance of the giant tree.

"Wow, this Nim Galuu seems very popular," said M.K.

"I thought this was a secret mission!" Grub said, a bit upset. "How many people did the queen tell about this?"

"Everyone's worried," said Ronin, "so they've come to Nim's."

"So he's like the wise old man of the forest?" M.K asked.

"More like the crazy uncle," responded Nod.

M.K. looked at him curiously as she, Nod, Ronin, Mub, and Grub entered the tree.

Inside, the Jinn were very worried.

"I hear the ceremony was attacked!"

"I hear the Boggans are taking over the forest! It's gonna be bad!"

"Nim Galuu will know what to do!" cried one of the Jinn.

Just then, a band began to play some mysterious music. A shadowy figure shrouded in fog rose from below. It was Nim Galuu, a caterpillar with a magician's flair. He was the go-to guy for reassurance, revelations, and a great party.

"Prepare to see your worries disappear!" exclaimed Nim. He waved his hand, making a moth disappear. "I know rumors have been flying!" He raised another hand, and the moth flew from his sleeve. Magic! "But the truth is never as bad as it seems. I have just returned from . . . the Rings of Knowledge!"

The crowd ooohed.

"Where every memory, every event that ever happened in the forest is recorded in these scrolls." He waved his hands and, magically, scrolls appeared in them. Just as he looked like he was about to read from

one of them, he cued the band and they picked up the tempo as he sang:

Listen party poopers, I've got something to say.
Dry your weeping eyes, we're gonna be OK.
So you don't have to worry about a doggone thing.
The Rings of Knowledge know everything.

The scrolls never lie and, honey, neither does Nim.
It's right here in my hands all six of them.
So tuck your little fears and put them right into bed.
It says right here that the queen has . . .

Nim unfurled the scroll and read the word "disappeared" to himself.

Nim started to sweat. He did not want his guests to know she had disappeared. The music vamped,

waiting for him to get to his big finale . . . and the crowd started to get restless, wondering what was going on.

The backup singers started singing, "Dry your weeping eyes, we're gonna be fine."

With the crowd distracted, Nim ran backstage. There he saw Ronin. "Ronin, did you hear about the queen? This is terrible!"

"I know—," said Ronin.

But Nim interrupted him and continued, "We gotta do something. We gotta keep everyone from freaking out."

"Yes," Ronin replied. "That's why—"

But before Ronin could finish his sentence, Nim continued, "We gotta make sure the royal pod is safe . . . far away and . . ."

Just then, Nim saw the pod in M.K.'s arms.

"What did you bring it here for?!" said Nim.

M.K. and Ronin looked at each other. "The queen's last words to me were 'bring the pod to Nim Galuu,'" M.K. said.

"Did she say anything else? Specific instructions? Maybe a note?" asked Nim.

"Those were her LAST WORDS before she disappeared. I thought you were magic?" said M.K.

"Magic might be stretching it," he replied. "I'm charismatic. Possibly charming."

Perking up, M.K. flat out asked, "Do you know what to do with the pod or not?"

"Not a clue," replied Nim. M.K. shot him a look and he continued, "But I *do* know where to look it up. Follow me!"

Nim led the group down a tunnel lit only by glowworms. They emerged into a vast space deep within the

tree. All around were ancient rings stuffed with scrolls.

"The Rings of Knowledge!" Grub exclaimed. "Is everything that happens really recorded here?"

"Oh, yeah," answered Nim.

"And you've read them all?" asked M.K.

"I've skimmed them," Nim said with a shrug.

"So is *this* event being recorded?" Grub asked.

"Of course," answered Nim.

"Is this?" asked Grub, this time making a silly, stretchy face.

This went on for a while until Nim tuned out the snail and continued looking for the scroll. "Blooming a pod . . . got to go way back for that."

When Nim finally found the right scroll, he unwound it and scanned it. "Okay, let's see. Pod, care of . . . must keep moist . . . oh, here we go. Well, the good news is, once the queen chooses

it, it's going to bloom no matter what."

Everyone thought that was great news.

"*But*," interrupted Nim, "it has to open tonight, in the light of the full moon, when it's at its highest peak. Mentions it a bunch of times."

"What happens if it blooms out of the moonlight?" asked Grub.

Nim read down the scroll to the jagged bottom edge. "Unclear. The last part's missing. Termites have been a problem." Then he brightened. "So, here I thought we were doomed! Celebration, anyone?"

Everyone left, except M.K.

"Wait," she said to Nim, who stopped to listen. "This is going to sound weird, but I'm not from this world. I thought maybe something in these scrolls could tell me how to get home."

"The scrolls don't tell us the future," Nim said.

"They only guide us with the knowledge of the past. Oh! That's a great line . . ."

"So you can't help me?" asked M.K.

"I didn't say that," replied Nim. He handed her an old, dusty scroll.

She unrolled it partway and found it covered in an ancient script. "I can't read this," M.K. told him.

"It's just dusty," said Nim, with a twinkle in his eye. "Blow it off."

So M.K. blew on the scroll, and a big cloud of dust flew off, transforming into an image—an image of Queen Tara!

"It's you!" M.K. cried.

M.K. was astonished at the figure of Tara standing in front of her.

"Come closer," the queen beckoned.

Suddenly, a giant shadow hovered over them.

M.K. turned to discover a giant-sized version of herself!

"It's a memory," M.K. realized. The memory of when she first stumbled upon this world of the Jinn.

"If you can hear me now, it means you got to Nim's," said the queen. "Today's not going the way I planned. The pod needs you."

"You don't understand," M.K. said desperately. "I have to get home. This has nothing to do with me."

"You're here for a reason," Queen Tara said. "Maybe you don't see the connections yet, but just because you don't see them doesn't mean they're not there. I know you're scared, but stay with the pod. Be with it when it blooms. And then, you'll get back what you've given."

The wind picked up, and the image of the queen began to fade again.

Professor Bomba is a scientist.
He believes tiny people live in the woods.

The forest folk do exist!
They are called the Jinn.

The Boggans are the
sworn enemy of the Jinn.

They want to destroy the forest by spreading rot and decay.

Nod is running for his life to escape a Boggan's poison arrow.

Nod is a Leafman—
although sometimes he
wishes he wasn't!

The Leafmen are brave Jinn soldiers who defend the forest.

Ronin is their
courageous leader.

Mandrake is the Boggans' leader and he has an evil plan.
He will steal the royal pod—the life force of the forest.

M.K. is a human girl who gets shrunk to Jinn size.
Now she must protect the pod.

Here are some other creatures who help protect the pod from the Boggans:

Mub and Grub

Nim Galuu

Mub, Nod, M.K., Ronin, and Grub will keep fighting to protect the pod and the life of the forest!

"Well, THAT was intense!" Nim exclaimed.

M.K. smiled to herself. "There's a way to get home. I have to be with the pod when it blooms, and that's tonight. Thank you!"

Nim smiled back. "I'm glad you were paying attention, because she started talking and woo . . ." He kept talking, but M.K. wasn't listening. She was filled with hope—finally.

When Ronin heard the news, he sprang into action. He pulled Nod aside and gave him very specific instructions: "We're not done until the pod blooms. I'm sending word to the Leafmen, so I need you to stay here and keep an eye on the pod."

A short while later, Ronin and Nim stood in the treetop with a group of fireflies.

"Let the Leafmen know that the pod is safe, and we're going to bloom it here," Ronin instructed.

Nim looked at the fireflies. "You heard him. Go tell 'em, boys!"

The fireflies launched into the sky to deliver their messages to the Leafmen.

Down below, Nod noticed M.K. returning from the Rings of Knowledge. He approached her. "Look, I'm thinking I didn't make the best first impression."

M.K. smiled. "It's okay. I've never had a guy fight a mouse for me before."

Relieved, Nod smiled, too. "You're not from around here, are you?"

"Not exactly," replied M.K. "But I have some time before I go back. Anything I should do?"

Nod grinned again. "You should give me a second chance."

M.K. agreed and held out her hand. "Deal." And to her surprise, Nod pulled her out of the window.

Once outside, Nod held a finger to his lips and pointed to a few moving shapes. They were barely visible through the thick fog. When it did clear, M.K. was stunned to see the shapes were actually a herd of deer. From her perspective, they were gigantic.

"Whoa," she said, astounded.

The deer passed by the pair, beautifully and slowly, before drifting back into the fog.

Nod smiled at her. "Put your arms around me," he told her. And soon they rode a deer's antlers while it wandered in the forest. They had no idea that in just a few moments, Mandrake would make his attack.

12

The ground below Nim's tree burst open and Mandrake emerged, sitting atop a star-nosed mole.

"Excuse me, but I've lost something very dear to me," he said mockingly. "It was left by a friend who's—" Then he spotted Mub and Grub with the pod. "You found it!"

"If you want to take this pod, you're going to have to go through us," Mub declared.

"Relax," said Mandrake. "I'm not going to hurt it. I need it alive."

Grub put his hands on his hips. "Well, we're the only ones who know how to keep it that way."

Mandrake smiled cruelly. "Thanks for the tip," he said, gesturing to his Boggan guards who grabbed Mub and Grub as he took the pod. They tossed the slug and the snail aboard the mole, and Mandrake spurred the animal back into its tunnel.

Ronin arrived a few seconds too late to do anything. He spotted Nod and M.K. entering through the window. Furious, Ronin stormed up to Nod and berated him for leaving the pod unattended.

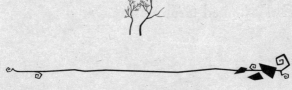

In Mandrake's lair, Mub and Grub huddled in a corner with the pod, surrounded by Boggans. Mandrake stood over them as he was giving a speech. He raised a spearlike object, and then Mub and Grub screamed.

"Please, stop!" begged Mub, in agony.

"My son was born on a night like this," Mandrake told them while holding a spiny nut he used as a memory box. He pulled out a set of pointy teeth. "These were his baby fangs. And here's the first skin he ever molted . . ."

"Your stories are boring and torturous!" Mub cried out.

Mandrake's eyes narrowed. "The Leafmen took my son from me. So I took something from them. It's basic etiquette: an eye . . ." He poked Grub in his eyestalk.

"Ow!" shouted Grub.

". . . for an eye," Mandrake finished, poking Mub in his eyestalk.

"Ow!" Mub moaned.

Mandrake sneered. "Tonight, your pod will bloom here. And what blooms in darkness, belongs to the darkness. So, soon I'll have another little dark prince. I'll destroy the forest with the very thing you hoped would save it."

"I hate to break it to you," said Grub. "But it doesn't say that in the scrolls."

A wicked smile crossed Mandrake's face. "It does in the part I have." He held up the piece of the scroll that was missing from Nim's.

Mub and Grub looked at each other. They knew they were in trouble, that the pod was in trouble, and they had no idea what to do next!

13

Back at Nim's oak, Ronin continued to berate Nod for leaving the pod. "Stay with the pod, that is all you had to do!"

"Yeah, but I just thought that—" Nod started to respond when Ronin continued, "Do you ever think about anyone besides yourself?"

M.K. stood up and took responsibility. "It wasn't all his fault," she said. "The queen gave it to me and I should have been with it."

"And you," Ronin said to M.K. "I expected as much from him, but I thought you would know better."

"We're really sorry," said Nod. "Okay, we just—"

"I don't want to hear it," Ronin said. "That was the last part of the queen that I—that any of us may ever have."

"I will do whatever it takes to help you get it back," M.K. promised him.

"I appreciate the enthusiasm," said Ronin as he saddled his bird. "But Wrathwood is too dangerous."

"You can't go alone," she insisted. "What about the whole leaves and tree thing that you said? Nim! Tell him!"

Nim tried to be reassuring. "Look, kid, the moon's

almost up. That's bloom-or-die time. So if no one has a better plan—"

"What if we sneak in, in disguise?" Nod suggested.

Ronin laughed and said sarcastically, "Great idea. I'll go as a grasshopper, and you can be my cricket lady friend." Then he added, "I don't have any Boggan armor handy, do you?"

M.K. piped up. "I know where we can get some." She then hopped on a bird and grabbed the reins. As Nod jumped on behind her, she said, "You might want to hang on."

M.K. spurred the bird into flight, a little shaky at first, but eventually got the hang of it. Nod held on tight, and Ronin followed behind, unsure of how he felt about the plan.

A short time later, M.K., Ronin, and Nod peered through the window of M.K.'s father's house.

"Over there," M.K. said, pointing to a display across the room. Boggan artifacts lined the shelves.

M.K. squeezed through the barely opened window, and Ronin and Nod followed.

From their perspective, the house was huge. To M.K., especially, it seemed like a brand-new place.

But there was no time to explore. They needed to get across the room to the shelves. Ronin leaped off the windowsill first.

Nod, wanting to show off, slid down an open tape measure, used the padded desk chair as a trampoline, and grabbed a cable to swing himself to the base of the shelves.

"Come on," he urged M.K.

She smiled, finally confident in her new size and skills. She stretched like an athlete, gave herself a running start, and jumped.

But she wasn't quite as successful as Nod. Instead, she bounced off the objects that Nod skillfully sprang from, logrolled on a couple of pencils, and ultimately landed with a *thud* on her bottom.

"That was awesome. Here," said Nod, extending his hand to help her up.

M.K. was embarrassed as she took his hand. Then she looked down to see her right leg was covered in a dust bunny—hair, lint, and other yucky stuff. She kicked at it, but it wouldn't come off. "Ew! That is some static cling!"

The more she tried to rub it off, the more static it became. She reached to brace herself on the metal wheel of the desk chair.

Nod shouted, "No, that's metal, don't touch tha—"

BLAM!

Because of her small size, the second M.K. touched the metal, the static shock blew her backward. She was out of the dust bunny, but her hair stood at attention.

Nod went to help her up again and received a little residual zap when he grabbed her hand. "Ow!"

"Knock it off," Ronin said seriously.

Nod and M.K. looked up to see Ronin already on the shelf above them. They climbed up to join him and took a closer look. They were amazed by what they saw: There were Boggan and Jinn artifacts all over the shelf, including bird-skull helmets and bat-skin clothes.

"You know, some of this stuff looks familiar," said Nod. "Hey!" He pulled a saddle down. "That's my saddle! Where are we?"

Suddenly, there was a *BOOM, BOOM, BOOM.*

They turned to see M.K.'s father, Bomba, walk past the doorway, holding an old shoebox. In their scale of time, he walked in slow motion.

"Ohhhh, it's where *this* guy lives!" Ronin said to M.K.

"I can't believe it!" added Nod. "He's been crashing around the forest like a bear for years. Most Stompers just come and go. But this guy's relentless."

"Stompers?" asked M.K.

"Yeah," replied Nod. "You know, like us, but big and dumb and slow. Always stomping on things . . . Stompers."

"And this one is obsessed with finding us," explained Ronin. "Obviously that's a security risk. Can't have one of his big fat feet stepping on Moonhaven."

Nod joined in. "One of his ginormous, flabby, dirty, stinky—"

"Okay! I got it!" M.K. said.

"So we've been throwing him off the trail," said Ronin.

M.K. looked puzzled. "You're just messing with him? But he's found all this stuff."

Ronin shook his head. "He only finds what we want him to find. Look at his map—we've got him looking everywhere but where we are." He pointed to an unmarked spot on Bomba's forest map, far away from the area with the pushpins clustered in it.

"I love how this guy talks," said Nod, adopting a much slower way of speaking. "Loook aaaat thisss flooowweerrr." He and Ronin cracked up.

M.K. was obviously not amused. "It's his life's work!"

But Nod and Ronin continued to make fun of Bomba. "IIIIIIIIIII hurrrrt myyyy ellbooooowwww!" Ronin cried.

"You're being idiots!" M.K. said. "He's my dad," she finally admitted.

Ronin and Nod instantly stopped goofing around.

"He's what?" said Nod.

"*I'm* a Stomper," said M.K.

Nod thought she was joking. "What happened? You got shrunk?"

"Yes," M.K. said, in all seriousness. She pointed to Ronin and added, "Which he knows!"

"Seriously?" Nod said to Ronin.

Ronin nodded. "It's been a weird day for everybody."

M.K. put her hands on her hips. "You got a problem with Stompers?"

Nod suddenly became somber. "A Stomper squashed my uncle."

"Oh my gosh! Really?" M.K. said, feeling terrible.

Nod grinned. "Nah, I'm just messing with you."

M.K. rewarded Nod with a swift shove, and Ronin couldn't help grinning. Then she turned and saw Bomba looking at some family pictures.

"I guess she's right about me," Bomba said sadly out loud. "All I seem to be able to do is drive people away."

"No, Dad! You didn't!" M.K. shouted. "I'm here!" Her angry words from that morning had affected him, and she'd do anything to take them back. But she couldn't. So she tried yelling again: "And you're right about all of it! Don't stop looking, not now!"

But Bomba didn't hear her. At most, if he listened

carefully, her voice would be a faint, high-pitched squeak.

However, someone else could hear those high-pitched squeaks . . .

14

Ozzy, sleeping at the top of the stairs, opened his eye. He couldn't recognize the squeaks he heard, but it was worth investigating. He turned to find a very small M.K. He barked and gave chase.

"Ozzy? Uh-oh!" M.K. exclaimed. She bolted off the steps, with the dog close behind. She ran toward

Ronin and Nod, who had collected Boggan armor to take with them.

When Nod saw what M.K. was running from, he spoke only one word: "Run!"

Bomba looked up to see what the commotion was about. "Ozzy?"

Ozzy barked again, followed by his customary sneeze and drool.

Bomba peeked in the doorway and addressed Ozzy. "Will you please stop—"

Right at that moment, out of the corner of his eye, Bomba spotted three tiny figures skittering across the floor.

"They're here! They're in my house!" Bomba shouted, overflowing with enthusiasm. He raced to the closet and grabbed a handheld vacuum. He had modified it by attaching a collection jar to it.

He quickly turned it on.

To M.K, Nod, and Ronin, the vacuum sounded like a hurricane. They scattered, as Bomba headed toward them. They tried to make it back to the window to escape, but Ozzy cut them off. Ronin aimed an arrow when—

"NO!" cried M.K. She gave him a shove and the errant arrow hit Bomba in the bottom.

"Ah!" cried Bomba. He swatted at the tiny arrow, as if it were a bee sting. He spun around, stumbled, and bumped his desk, knocking Nod off it. "Ow! I hurt myyyyyy elbowwww!"

"Did you hear that? He said it!" Nod said excitedly. Then Nod hit the floor, looking up in time to see Bomba's coffee cup falling straight for him! He dove to the side, just as the cup smashed down, spilling coffee all over the floor.

When Ronin made it back to the windowsill, he

immediately cut off part of the cord from the blinds. He tied and secured it around a slat, tossing the other end to Nod and M.K.

Nod and M.K. spotted the cord and sprinted for it. Nod scurried up the cord to where Ronin was waiting. The two Leafmen prepared to pull up M.K. next, but as she grabbed the cord, the suction from Bomba's vacuum pulled her back!

"No!" shouted Nod. "Don't let go! Don't let go!"

M.K. held on while Ronin and Nod pulled on the cord. But it was no use. M.K was sucked into the vacuum, landing hard inside the collection jar.

Bomba held the jar up to his face, adjusting his buffering equipment so he was able to see the tiny creature better. "Hello there, my little friend." He looked closer and saw a two-inch-tall M.K. staring back at him.

"Dad! Dad!" M.K. shouted, banging on the glass.

Bomba's eyes went wide, he turned pale, and then he fainted.

The jar went crashing to the floor, breaking open and freeing M.K.

"Dad!" M.K. called again. She reached out to touch him, wishing she could explain.

Ronin interrupted her thoughts. "Let's go."

Nod noticed M.K. was torn. "You can't stay," he told her gently. "You're with us now. Come on, we've got to go."

M.K. knew Nod was right. The pod was still in danger. But before she left, she placed a red pin on Bomba's map revealing Moonhaven's location. Then she grabbed on to the cord and was hauled up to the windowsill.

As they left the house, M.K. asked, "You think he's okay?"

"He'll be fine," said Nod. "Their heads are like rocks." Then he quickly added, "Uh . . . smart rocks!"

Not long after, a full moon began to rise as M.K., Ronin, and Nod stood on a branch looking down on the gnarled stump of Wrathwood. It would take all their bravery and courage to fight the Boggans and reclaim the pod before it began to bloom.

They fastened their Boggan armor around them.

"That's a whole lot of ugly," Nod said, looking at M.K.'s bird-skull helmet.

"Ugh," said M.K. "It smells like something died in here."

"Something did," Ronin pointed out, and M.K. made a face.

They headed toward the stump, surrounded by Boggans in every direction.

"How do we know where to go?" Nod asked.

"I've been here before," replied Ronin. "With your father."

Nod looked surprised. "He never told me about this."

"He never got the chance," Ronin said sadly.

At that moment, Nod began to look at Wrathwood with new eyes, knowing he was following in his father's footsteps.

Ronin led the others through a tunnel, their Boggan disguises keeping them from standing out.

M.K. had to stifle her scream when she came face-to-face with a bat. Looking up, she saw hundreds of bats lining the ceiling, sleeping fitfully.

At the end of the tunnel, the trio found themselves

overlooking the heart of Wrathwood—a giant, multi-leveled coliseum. Above this arena, there was a crack in the ceiling, revealing a sliver of sky.

Ronin pointed to the crack. "There's our exit. Meet me back here when you've got the pod and the slugs."

"What? How are we going to find them?" asked Nod.

Ronin pointed to a wet, glistening trail leading down a tunnel guarded by two Boggans. "Follow the slime." He began to walk the other way.

"Aren't you coming with us?" asked M.K.

"I'm going to make sure nobody follows you," Ronin told them.

M.K. and Nod looked at each other, visibly worried.

Ronin reassured them. "Don't worry, you get the easy part. I get the fun part." He faced the

Boggans and pulled off his disguise. "Hey, look! It's a Leafman!" he shouted.

The Boggans looked around, confused.

Ronin rolled his eyes. He couldn't believe how thickheaded the Boggans were when Mandrake wasn't around. He called to them again: "I'll keep this simple. I run. You try to catch me."

The Boggans finally caught on, and they swarmed to attack. With precision, Ronin successfully started taking them out, as Nod and M.K. headed off in search of Mub, Grub, and the pod.

M.K. and Nod followed the slime trail until suddenly a horde of Boggans came bustling down the tunnel. They were on their way to fight Ronin. Nod and M.K. pushed their way upstream against the crowd until they made it through to the other side.

"When I get big again," began M.K., "I am so

coming back here with a can of bug spray!"

Hurriedly, they ran down a path until the slime stopped at a dismembered jawbone, lying on its side.

"Mub? Grub?" M.K. called quietly.

Mub's eyestalks popped up from under the jawbone. "We're down here! I knew you'd come!" Then he turned to Grub, and added, "See? That girl is smitten."

Nod pushed the jawbone away and he and M.K. retrieved the pod, as well as Mub and Grub.

"Hurry, before the guards come back!" urged M.K.

But it was too late. They could hear Boggans coming down the corridor.

"I have a plan!" said Grub.

Two Boggan guards entered to find the jawbone moved and the room empty. Suddenly, one of them

was hit on the head with a drop of slime. They looked up to see M.K. and Nod on the snail and slug, all making their escape!

"Go, go, go!" yelled Nod.

"Ow! That hurts!" complained Mub. Nod was holding on to Mub's eyestalks so he wouldn't fall off.

The snail and slug crawled across the ceiling, staying just out of reach of the pursuing Boggans.

Meanwhile, the number of Boggans chasing Ronin had increased tenfold. But they were no closer to catching him as Ronin leaped from ledge to ledge, always managing to stay ahead of the swarm.

Suddenly, the Boggans retreated. But they weren't fleeing; they were clearing a path for their boss, Mandrake.

"Ronin, what a surprise," said Mandrake. "I get so few guests."

The Leafman shrugged. "It could be the stench of death. Some people don't care for it," Ronin said.

The Boggans watching clearly didn't like that, but Mandrake motioned for them to stand down. "It's all right. Ronin's an old . . . what do you call someone you've known for a long time and always wanted to kill? Wait, it'll come to me."

"I hope it comes to you quickly. You don't have much more time," said Ronin.

Mandrake jumped down and took out the bridge Ronin was standing on. The Leafman barely leaped to safety.

Ronin swung, but Mandrake blocked the attack.

"I expected you'd come, but I didn't think you'd come alone," said Mandrake.

"Who said I'm alone?" Ronin replied. He knew that Mandrake didn't see M.K., Nod, Mub, and Grub

up above, making their way along the ceiling into the coliseum toward the exit. Unfortunately, the two guards pursued them.

Nod swung his foot—and it connected with the two Boggans!

Just as Mandrake was going to deliver a crushing blow to Ronin, the two guards landed directly on his head. Mandrake looked up to see M.K. and Nod riding the slug and snail and let out a primal roar. Thousands of Boggans poured out of the walls, climbing toward M.K. and Nod. Mandrake leaped up the walls to block the exit.

Ronin looked down below and saw Boggans pouring out of every hole, getting closer and closer. He pursued Mandrake as the Boggan leader went after Nod and M.K. Ronin leaped in and grabbed Mandrake by the neck. They tumbled down together,

hitting a ledge. Mandrake was knocked off into a pit of Boggans. Ronin held onto the ledge with one hand.

"Ronin! Hang on!" shouted Nod.

Ronin climbed up on the ledge, just as the Boggan swarm arrived. The Leafman began hand-to-hand combat, launching punches left and right.

"Go! Take the pod to Moonhaven!" Ronin ordered Nod.

"I'm not leaving without you!" Nod insisted.

"Now you sound like a Leafman!" Ronin said proudly. Then he was swallowed up in the teeming mass of Boggans below.

"Ronin!" exclaimed Nod.

M.K. touched Nod's arm and motioned to the exit. "Come on."

Nod took one last look at Ronin. He didn't want

to leave him, but he knew they didn't have much time. The Boggans wouldn't be far behind, and they needed to get the pod back to Moonhaven before the moon reached its highest peak. Along with Mub and Grub, M.K. and Nod hopped onto Nod's waiting sparrow and flew off, worrying and wondering how Ronin was going to fight off all those Boggans—and knowing that he probably wouldn't.

16

As the group flew closer to Moonhaven, a squadron of Leafmen came out to meet them.

"We've been waiting for you," said the squadron leader. "Where's Ronin?"

Nod hesitated. "He . . . uh . . . gave us a head start."

All the Leafmen understood what that meant. Immediately, they escorted Nod and the others through a gap in the trees, revealing Moonhaven, glowing in the moonlight.

M.K.'s eyes went wide. She had seen many new and amazing things that day, but Moonhaven took her breath away. It was unlike anything she could have predicted or imagined. In the center, she could see a crowd of Jinn. M.K. held up the pod for them to see, and the Jinn cheered.

Nim greeted them, arms open, delighted to see them and the pod. "You guys made it!" He led them inside to the royal chamber and placed the pod on a pedestal where the moonlight would shine on it through a window.

Mub and Grub pushed through the crowd to get front-row seats.

"Do you know what this means?" Grub excitedly asked Mub.

"We single-handedly saved the forest!" answered Mub. "Eye-five!"

Nod shook his head, then noticed that M.K. was hanging back a bit. Cautiously, he approached her and said, "So when the pod opens . . ."

M.K. nodded. "I think the power of it will . . ."

"Send you home," Nod finished, realizing the gravity of what that would mean.

M.K. looked up at Nod and could see that he didn't want her to go. She sighed, not knowing how she could say good-bye.

The pod began to glow, reacting to the moonlight. Everyone gathered close, with hopes and futures all dependent on the successful blooming of the pod.

Suddenly, the moonlight started to flicker. Then

it went out! The pod started to wilt. What was happening?

A screeching sound could be heard, and the Leafmen looked up to see Mandrake's bats blocking the moonlight from entering the window.

Mandrake himself flew on a black grackle, watching and insuring that the pod would bloom in darkness. But strangely, the bats weren't descending.

"I don't think they're attacking," said M.K. "They're blocking out the moon!"

Nod and the Leafmen took to the sky, heading directly for the bats. He looked at the Leafmen on both sides of him, realizing they were flying together as a team. He knew this was what Ronin would have wanted. Lifted by the feeling, Nod spurred his bird higher.

Down below in the royal chamber, M.K. anxiously

watched the sky as the Leafmen pushed a hole through the blanket of bats. For a moment, the moonlight returned . . . but it immediately closed back up.

M.K. wanted to help. She spotted a sword and tried picking it up. But it was so heavy, she could only drag it.

Nim chuckled. "What are you doing?"

"I'm going to help," M.K. said to Nim.

"Whoa, whoa, you heard the queen. If you want to get home, you have to be here with the pod when it blooms. Isn't that what you want?" said Nim.

"So I should just sit here?" M.K. responded.

"I didn't say that," replied Nim.

"So I should go up there?" M.K. was starting to get frustrated.

"Didn't say that either," replied Nim.

Now completely frustrated, M.K. said, "Just tell me what you ARE saying!"

"I'm saying, who gives up everything for a world that's not even theirs?"

M.K. had a moment of realization. "My dad does. I have to get my dad." She headed for the exit.

Nim called after her, "Where do you think you're going?"

M.K. exclaimed, "The queen said I was here for a reason. This must be it!"

She hopped aboard a sparrow and zoomed away under the shadow of the bats. She just hoped her plan would work.

Nod and the Leafmen continuously attacked the bats, while Boggans swirled all around, their warrior cries mingling with the shrieks of the bats.

It was apparent that the Leafmen were losing. The swarm of bats was just too massive. Other bats immediately closed every hole the Leafmen opened.

Back inside the royal chamber, Mub stood next to the pod. Suddenly, the wilted pod began to open.

"The pod!" he exclaimed. "It's blooming in darkness." He looked up to watch the battle above, hoping for a miracle.

But the bats continued to fly above Moonhaven, blocking out the moon.

Then a new fighter rose, careening wildly through the air, bobbing and weaving. He wore a Leafman helmet and cried, "Upward, brave steed! Into the fray!"

It was Grub!

At the same time, Nod was continuing to fight his way through the swarm of bats, and he was in trouble: one of the Boggans was about to take out Nod. Suddenly, a surprise guest took the Boggan out for him: Bufo!

Nod was shocked to see the shady, toadlike Jinn again. "What are you doing here?" he asked.

"Hey, it's my forest, too," replied Bufo. "Plus I have money on the Leafmen—and I hate to lose!"

He motioned behind him, and Nod turned to see the jockeys from the bird race. They were following Bufo into battle. Nod grinned. They were all on the same side now.

As Mandrake headed toward the pod, Nod and the racers fought back, flying circles around him, dizzying his grackle, blocking its every path.

But a squadron of Boggans swooped down, knocking the jockeys out of the sky.

Grub came to the rescue—accidentally—as the jockeys all landed on Grub's flailing bird. The racers thanked Grub for saving their lives.

"A Leafman finds a way!" Grub proudly answered.

Meanwhile, trying to get closer to Mandrake, Nod leaped off his bird and onto a bat. Mandrake

swung his club at him.

"Missed me!" Nod said tauntingly.

"I wasn't aiming for you," Mandrake replied.

Nod looked down to see his bat aging quickly and horribly—shriveling, molting, and finally reduced to only bones. Nod rode the bones as they plummeted to the forest floor.

He survived the impact, but he was a long distance away now. He looked up to see Mandrake entering Moonhaven. Nod ran as fast as he could. He had to defeat Mandrake before the pod bloomed!

Inside his house, a shaft of moonlight hit Bomba in the eye, waking him up from where he had fainted on the floor. He sat up, bleary-eyed, and looked at

the shattered collection jar, then at all his equipment, specimens, and sketches.

"They're all right about me," Bomba said sadly to Ozzy. "All these years, chasing things that aren't there. I actually thought I saw my daughter, two inches tall, stuck in a bug jar. I've lost my mind." Then he shook his head. "And I'm talking to a dog."

Ozzy barked, sneezed, and drooled in response.

Meanwhile, out in the dark forest, M.K. flew from Moonhaven, fearless and focused. She spotted a red light. It was one of Bomba's cameras. She flew to it, and the camera turned itself on from her movement.

"Dad! Hey! Dad! I need your help!" she yelled, waving her arms.

But then the light on the camera went out.

M.K. wasn't sure what happened, so she spurred the bird on and flew to another camera. "Dad, look at

me! I'm right here. Just check your cameras!"

That camera shut down, as well.

When the last camera turned off, M.K. was distraught. "Dad, please! I need you!"

But Bomba was shutting down all of his equipment, giving up his life's work. He shoved stuff into boxes, only stopping when something caught his eye. A red pushpin on his forest map had been moved. Now it was stuck in the actual location of Moonhaven. Bomba looked hard, trying to make sense of it.

Meanwhile, out in the darkness, M.K. felt very alone. She looked back at the moon, seeing the swarming bats, feeling like she failed.

Thwack!

Apparently she wasn't alone! A Boggan and his arrows bore down on her. She took off through the woods aboard her bird.

"I am *so* over Boggans," she muttered. She ripped an acorn from a tree and hurled it at him. It whacked him across the face, but it didn't deter him. It just made him angrier.

The Boggan hovered over her and drew his bow. M.K. winced, preparing for the kill shot when—

Chomp! The Boggan was gone!

M.K. turned to see Ozzy shaking the Boggan in his mouth. "Ozzy!" Then she looked up and happily yelled, "Dad!"

In full expedition gear, Bomba headed through the woods, clutching the map. Ozzy ran circles around him, barking excitedly. When Bomba stopped to get his bearings, a bird stopped in front of his face, startling him. He reached for it, and M.K. jumped off the bird and landed in his hand.

"Don't faint!" M.K. said slowly and loudly.

"I won't," Bomba replied.

"How did you find me?" asked M.K.

Bomba held up the red pushpin and smiled. "I got your message!"

"You were right. They're real," M.K. told him.

The bats shrieked overhead, reminding M.K. of the important business at hand.

"And they need your help!" called M.K. "Follow me!"

She jumped back on her bird and led Bomba to Moonhaven. Hopefully, they weren't too late!

18

Bomba stood outside Moonhaven, his eyes wide with wonder.

"It's all real," he said, amazed. "It's really here."

M.K. hovered in front of him, trying to get his attention. "Dad! The bats—we have to get them away from the moon!"

But Bomba was too captivated by Moonhaven. "It's so beautiful."

M.K. knew time was running out. She jumped into Bomba's pocket and pulled out his mp3 player. She scrolled through his playlist until she found what she was looking for: "bat calls."

"Oh, you want me to play the frequencies that attract the bats?" he asked.

M.K. jumped on the play button. Out came a noise that sounded like a high-pitched screech to humans, but to Jinn-sized creatures, it sounded like a low thrumming. It began to attract the attention of the bats. They flew toward the sound; they flew toward Bomba and opened up the moonlight!

With Leafman-like agility, M.K. sprang out of Bomba's hand and aboard her bird again. "I'll find you, Dad," she called out to him as the bats

swarmed her father.

Inside the royal chamber, another battle began brewing. Mandrake had burst into the room on his grackle. A stream of arrows was unleashed, but Mandrake swung his club and batted them away. The Leafmen kept attacking, but Mandrake struck the floor with his club, sending blight to take them down.

Mandrake looked up to see Nim, with Mub behind him, protecting the pod.

"This must be the delivery room," he said, chuckling wickedly.

"Whoa, boy, are *you* lost!" Nim said, trying to lighten the mood. "Down the hall, make a left, and—"

Mandrake shoved Nim and the slug out of the way and reached for the pod. "My dark prince. Come to Daddy."

But the pod's tendrils shrank from his touch.

Then Ronin stepped out of the shadows. "I don't think it likes you."

Excited to see his hero, Mub shouted out, "Ronin!"

"Then again, I don't really care for you myself," said Ronin. He advanced, wounded and beaten up, but ready for one last stand. Mandrake snarled and furiously attacked. Ronin responded, but it was clear he was weak, and probably wouldn't last long in his condition.

"When I left you for dead, I thought you would stay that way," Mandrake snarled.

"It's going to take more than a few thousand Boggans to get rid of me," replied Ronin.

"Then why don't I take another crack at it," said Mandrake. He pinned Ronin to the floor, and without

his sword the Leafman was defenseless.

"What's that little saying you people have?" said Mandrake, as he hovered over Ronin. "'Lots of leaves, something something'? Very inspiring." He raised his club. "But in the end, every leaf falls and dies alone."

Mandrake brought his club down, but a sword blocked the strike!

"No one is alone," said Nod, revealing himself holding the sword. He looked at Ronin. "Not even him."

At that moment, an army of Leafmen dropped from the sky and surrounded Mandrake. Moonlight began to stream back into the royal chamber, where it struck the pod, causing it to burst open. A bright light erupted, hitting Mandrake and hurling him out of the chamber and into a tree.

"Nooooo!" cried Mandrake as he landed in his own poisonous rot, which instantly enveloped him whole. Mandrake was finally destroyed by the very thing he loved so much—decay!

M.K. ran toward Moonhaven, looking toward the moonlight bathing the night sky. She was relieved to have helped save Moonhaven, but she knew it was too late to save herself and return home. When she reached the royal chamber, she stood in the back and watched.

Nod, Ronin, and the Leafmen approached the open pod, wondering about the glow inside. Many Jinn watched, including the mother and daughter Jinn from the pod-selection ceremony. A wind blew through, lifting the glowing flecks of light out of the pod. The Leafmen and all of the Jinn watched as the swirl of light reached the Jinn daughter, who was standing with her mother. The light formed into the image of Queen Tara.

The queen pressed a cheek close to the Jinn daughter's ear and whispered, "Look after them for me." Then she embraced the girl and dissolved into a bright burst of light.

When the light subsided, the Jinn daughter had been transformed into the new queen, with crown and cape. Her mother was shocked.

"Your Majesty," Nim Galuu said immediately.

The Jinn all around fell to their knees and bowed.

Off to the side, Nod caught Ronin's eye.

"You look terrible," Nod told him.

Ronin grinned. "Hey, did you see how many times I got hit? I learned that from you."

Nod grinned back. "You're not going to make me say all the stuff I learned from you now, are you?"

"Well, you'd have learned a whole lot more from your dad," said Ronin. "I was a pretty poor substitute."

Nod shook his head. "Don't beat yourself up. Lately you've shown some real promise."

Ronin couldn't help but laugh.

"Oh, please, just say you love each other," M.K. interjected.

Ronin exchanged a confused look with Nod. "I thought we just did."

Just then Nod realized M.K. was still there—and not big again! He was happy to see her, but he could tell she was trying to put on a brave face.

"I'm sorry," Nod offered. "But not completely sorry." He reached out to her, but M.K. started to rise off the ground.

"What's happening?" M.K. asked, a little concerned.

"A queen brought you here," explained Nim, "How about a queen sends you back?" He gestured to the new queen, her eyes closed in concentration, thrilled to be using her new power.

"It's working!" the new queen said excitedly.

M.K. looked sadly at Ronin and Nod. "I have to say good-bye."

"What for? You're part of us," Ronin said.

M.K. remembered the "Many leaves, one tree"

motto and felt slightly better. She asked Nod to put his arms around her, to keep her from floating away. Then she kissed him, as they became enveloped in tendrils of bright light, until no one could see them anymore.

Bomba stood in the forest, thinking about the events of the past few hours. His life's work—everything that had ever mattered to him—was real. And his daughter had shown him the proof. He felt a pang of regret that M.K. wasn't here with him now. Where was she? Would he get to thank her for leading him to the Jinn? But more important than that, he wanted a fresh start, and a real chance for them to get to know each other.

The sound of leaves rustling pulled Bomba from his thoughts. He looked up and gasped.

M.K. was standing in front of him, back to her normal size. She smiled. Bomba smiled, too. They were going to get their chance after all! M.K. ran up to her father and gave him a hug.

Ozzy peeked over a bush, then barked, sneezed, and drooled. He ran past them and then doubled back, running in happy circles at the reunion.

Now Bomba had someone to share his research with. And it wasn't just anyone, it was his daughter! M.K. was a great guide to the world of the Jinn! When they got back to the house, M.K. watched over her father's shoulder as he furiously scribbled in a journal.

"Well, what do you think?" he asked finally, show-ing a naturalist's sketch of a Leafman warrior.

M.K. looked closely at the drawing, admiration

showing on her face. "It's perfect, Dad." Then she added, "Except the boots are higher, and the sleeves are longer. And they wear actual helmets, not acorns."

"Really? Well, they should seriously consider the potential!" said Bomba. He pinned up the drawing next to the many other sketches of the Jinn.

Ozzy ran up to M.K, panting happily.

"Here you go, boy," M.K. said. "Grr!" She tossed a small, hand-sewn Boggan toy. Ozzy happily grabbed it in his mouth and shook it.

Suddenly a *beep beep beep* echoed through the house. M.K. jumped up and began to run into the other room, then stopped herself, remembering it was her dad's equipment.

Bomba smiled. "Go. It's always for you, anyway." He couldn't be happier to have someone as fascinated by this world of tiny people as he was.

M.K. raced into the other room and sat down at a computer. She instantly smiled at the image on the screen: a forest-cam view of Nod. He was wearing a Leafman uniform and practicing a few sword moves.

"Hey," said M.K.

"Hey," said Nod.

"How's work?" she asked.

"It's not work when you love your job," replied Nod. "'Many leaves, one tree,' that's what I always say."

"Uh-huh," M.K. said, smiling to herself, remembering how Nod *used* to feel about being a Leafman. It was wonderful to see that he had learned what it meant to be part of a team.

"What do you think you're doing, leaf boy?" Mub said to Nod.

"Leafman," Nod corrected. "You know it's Leafman."

"Hi, Mub," M.K. replied.

"*We* were talking," Nod said to Mub, trying to get rid of him.

"There's a big sack of shut-your-flat-face over there by that tree," Mub told Nod. "Why don't you go pick it up?"

"Listen, slick—"

"Guys, don't fight," M.K. said.

"Oh, it won't be a fight," Mub clarified. "I could whip him with both eyes behind my back."

"I'd like to see you try, jelly butt!" Nod said confidently.

The next instant, Mub scrunched down and opened his mouth wide. *Gulp!*

"Ew!" said M.K., hearing Nod's muffled screams.

"Not so tough now," Mub said to Nod.

"Mub! Get him out of your mouth," M.K. said.

She sighed, then got up from the desk and quickly found her father. "Dad, I've got to go Heimlich my friend out of a slug."

Bomba looked over her shoulder at the monitor. "Yeah, that looks pretty weird." Turning back to M.K., he added, "Here, don't forget this."

He plopped a tricked-out helmet on her head. She thanked him with a kiss on the cheek.

"Tell them about the acorn helmets," he called after her.

M.K. paused. "Or you could tell them yourself?" she suggested.

Bomba's face lit up with excitement. He slapped on a helmet of his own. Then he and M.K. ran out the door and into the forest, with Ozzy following behind—barking, sneezing, and drooling all the way.